KT-450-362

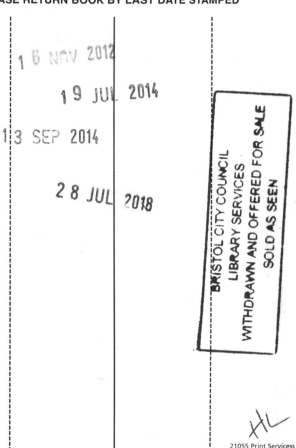

For my lovely nephew, Leo
K.D.

For Tom
M.B.

Reading Consultant: Prue Goodwin, Lecturer in literacy and children's books

ORCHARD BOOKS
338 Euston Road, London NW1 3BH
Orchard Books Australia
Level 17/207 Kent Street, Sydney, NSW 2000

First published in 2012
First paperback publication in 2013

ISBN 978 1 40831 216 2 (hardback)
ISBN 978 1 40831 224 7 (paperback)

A CIP catalogue record for this book is available
from the British Library.

1 3 5 7 9 10 8 6 4 2 (hardback)
1 3 5 7 9 10 8 6 4 2 (paperback)

Printed in Great Britain

Orchard Books is a division of Hachette Children's Books,
an Hachette UK company.

www.hachette.co.uk

Fairy Tale Twists

Jack to the Rescue!

Written by Katie Dale
Illustrated by Matt Buckingham

ORCHARD

Far away, a long time back,
there lived a lad whose name was Jack.
His head was filled with plans and dreams,
and countless money-making schemes...
He'd been a spy,

a pilot,

jester...

…a parachute and toffee-tester.

"You can't get rich quick, lad – that's crazy!"
Jack's mum said. "Go sell our Daisy."

Jack walked a while, then met Bo Peep.
"Oh crumbs!" she wailed. "I've lost
my sheep!"

"I'll help!" Jack cried. "They can't be far!"
And sure enough, just then – "**Baa-baa!**"

"My lamb!" cried Bo.

                    "He's not," said Mary
(who always had to be contrary).
She blew her horn – the lamb chased after.
Mary Mary roared with laughter.

"See?" she smirked. "He's my lamb now.
Unless, of course, you'll swap your cow?"

"Daisy?" Poor Jack gasped in shock —
then looked at Bo, who'd lost her flock.
Jack sighed. "I want the horn then, too."
They sealed the deal, and then Jack
BLEW!

At once Bo's sheep came flocking back!
"Hurray!" Bo cried. "Oh thank you, Jack!"
"As your reward, please take this wool
from Baa-Baa Black Sheep – three
bags full."

Jack waved goodbye, then passed a tuffet,
where he found distraught Jill Muffet!
"Help!" she squealed, for there beside her
sat the **MOST ENORMOUS** spider!

Jack paled, but then heard Humpty yell:
"He can't stand water – here's a well!"

So Jack and Jill raced up the hill
and filled the bucket up until—

Quite suddenly Jill Muffet slipped!
Jack tried to catch her – but he tripped!

As the bucket splashed about,
the spider scrambled up the spout!

Poor Humpty Dumpty leapt in fright!
He couldn't keep himself upright!
He slipped and tumbled off the wall.
Jack saw Humpty start to fall...

and threw his wool sacks on the ground,
so Humpty landed safe and sound.

"Whew!" cried Humpty. "Thank you, Jack!
However can we pay you back?
Come, have some pudding!"

Jack smiled. "Yum!"
He pulled a plum out with his thumb!

But then he got an awful shock,
as three blind mice ran up the clock –
then quickly chased the farmer's wife!
Jill sighed. "Those rodents plague
   my life!"

Jack smiled. "I might have an idea
to make your vermin disappear..."

Jack blew his horn, and every mouse
then followed him out of the house...

and up the street, past girls and boys,
who quickly dropped their books
and toys...

…and followed Jack across the brook.

The little bridge beneath them shook.

A troll jumped out! **"GET OFF MY HOUSE!"**

The children fled – and every mouse!

But Jack just frowned. "Mate, what's
the matter?"
"You folk – and goats! You stamp
and clatter!
I haven't slept a wink all week!"

Said Jack: "Wait – let me take a peek…"

He stuffed some wool between the planks,
and made them silent!

Troll laughed. "Thanks!"

"Well, clever boy!" an old hag said.
"But can you build with gingerbread?
I'll pay you if you lend a hand."
The house Jack built was very grand…

"Now here's your pay." She gave him beans!
Jack groaned. He needed cash, not greens!
The hag just grinned. "They may look old,
but they'll be worth their weight in gold!"

Jack's skills spread quickly far and wide.
"Mum will be proud of me!" he cried.

"We all need homes!" cried out three pigs.
So Jack built homes:

straw...

bricks...

and twigs.

But when a wolf came to the door,
two of the homes fell to the floor!

Jack's business shut: his dream had failed.
And as he wandered home, it hailed.

"We need a house!" a small voice cried.

"I'm closed, I'm sorry," Jack replied.

"Oh please!" the elves begged. "We are lost!

We need to shelter from the frost!"

"Here," Jack smiled. "Come, use my welly.

It's dry and warm – though might be smelly!"

"Thank you, Jack!" the elves replied.

Eagerly they climbed inside.

Jack did his best to make it cosy,
then he started feeling dozy…

When Jack woke up he rubbed his eyes,
and looked around in sheer surprise –

Surrounding him were lots of shoes!
All different styles, and shapes, and hues!

A note read:

Jack, you were so kind,
we thought we elves
should help you find
your new job – making
shoes to sell.
We've made a start.
Thank you. Farewell!

Jack's stylish footwear hit the news —
soon *everybody* wanted shoes!
Wooden clogs…

and glassy slippers…

dancing shoes…

and boots…
and flippers!

The king himself soon came to call.
"I need an outfit for the ball!
And matching boots!" His Highness said.
Jack made a dazzling suit of red.

"What *purr*fect boots!" A cat walked in.

"They're sold," Jack said. "They're for
the king."

"I've gold," Puss said.

"No, thanks," said Jack.

Puss hissed at him. "Then watch your back!"

Jack worked and worked, and then
dropped off,
till he was woken by a cough...

The king was there! "I LOVE my suit!
But tell me, lad, where are my boots?"
Jack looked around him in despair –
the scarlet boots he'd made weren't there!

The king frowned. "All your boots are black!
I told you they must all match, Jack!
Guards!" he cried. "Off with his head!"
"That's not your suit!" Jack quickly said.

Jack racked his brain. "Your suit's just there!"
His Highness turned and looked round.
  "Where?"
For Jack was pointing to thin air!
Jack smiled. "This cloth is very rare…
For only clever men can see it.
Try it on – I guarantee it!"

The king turned to his servant. "Well?"
"Your Majesty, I think it's swell!"

"It's gorgeous!" cried the guards. "It's cool!"
For no one wants to seem a fool!
"I'll wear it home!" the king cried. "Great!"
"No, no!" Jack called out, just too late…

For everybody turned to stare.

The king's smile faltered. Someone laughed.
And then he started feeling daft.
"Guards!" he yelled. "Off with Jack's head!"
Poor frightened Jack turned fast – and fled!

Jack was nimble, Jack was quick,
he ran right past the house of brick.

He crossed the stream and reached
the shore,
when suddenly, behind him – "ROAR!"

The king's guards scattered, terrified.
"Hurry, Jack!" the old troll cried.

Humpty Dumpty saw them all,
and quickly jumped straight off his wall!

All the king's horses and all the king's men stopped to put him together, but then – the Duke of York's ten thousand men marched up the hill – then down again!

"Jack, blow your horn!" called out Bo Peep.
At once the road was filled with sheep!
And rats and mice and children too!
The angry troop could not get through!

"My son!" Jack's mother cried. "Oh Jack!
We're out of cash – thank God you're back!
The fridge is bare, the cupboards too,
the roof's come down, our rent is due!
Tell me, how much did you make?"
Jack showed her.

"Oh, for goodness' sake!
Three mouldy beans?" She threw them out –
but then the beans began to sprout!

"There he is!" a soldier cried.
Jack looked round for a place to hide…
Then climbed the beanstalk, leaf by leaf.
He stared around in disbelief.
Before him stood a house of gold
while all around was icy cold.

Then came a roar: "**FEE! FI! FO! FUM!**"
"Help!" thought Jack. "I want my mum!"

A giant entered. **"FO! FUM! FEE!**
How dare you come to steal from me!
Wait a minute – what's that noise?"
The garden filled with girls and boys!

Jack wailed: "They must have followed me!"
But then the giant laughed in glee!
For as the kids began to sing
the flowers bloomed!
　　　　"They've brought back spring!
For years my life's been icy cold
and all I cared about was gold!"

"But now you've brought me so much joy –
however can I thank you, boy?
Perhaps some gold? Or diamond rings?"

Jack and his mum could live like kings!
That's what they'd wanted all along!
But wait – for what if they were wrong…?

For all their gold and endless treasure
had not brought king or giant pleasure...

Then Jack recalled the small elves who
had been contented with a shoe...

Jack chose his prize and home he went,
and found his life was quite content.
For who needs gold, or suits, or wealth,
if you have food, a house, and health…
and friends? For when Jack played, the sound
brought folk to dance from miles around.

And all the king's horses and all the
   king's men
never came looking for Jack there again…

Fairy Tale Twists

Written by Katie Dale
Illustrated by Matt Buckingham

All priced at £4.99

Orchard Books are available from all good bookshops,
or can be ordered from our website, www.orchardbooks.co.uk,
or telephone 01235 827702, or fax 01235 827703.